ROYALTY

DAKIARA

MIND FLOW PUBLISHING & PRODUCTION, LLC.

CONTENTS

1. Chapter One — 1
2. Chapter Two — 9
3. Chapter Three — 15
4. Chapter Four — 25
5. Chapter Five — 32
6. Chapter Six — 39
7. Chapter Seven — 45
8. Chapter Eight — 49
9. Chapter Nine — 55
10. Chapter Ten — 58

Thank You for Reading! — 63
Coming Soon! — 65
Flint (Available Soon!) — 67
About the Author — 69

First Printing: 2020

ISBN 978-1-951271-13-8 Paperback

ISBN 978-1-951271-12-1 Ebook

Additional copies of this book and others are available by mail or by visiting the website listed below. Check website for pricing.

Mind Flow Publishing & Production LLC

PO Box 48768 Cumberland, North Carolina 28331-8768

www.mindflowpublishingproduction.com

Cover design by Covers in Color

Editing by Stories Matter Editing

Formatting Design by Clarity Townsend

Thank you for helping to bring Royalty to life......

ROYALTY

CHAPTER ONE

"*E*lle, you must finish getting packed, we will be leaving for St. Martin's University tomorrow at 7 a.m. You know I hate to be late."

Elle was forever a procrastinator. Elaina knew there was no helping her child. *If only my mom understood. I'm not going to fit in. I'm not like them.* Elle had always felt inferior to others when it meant comparing herself to almost anyone. St. Martin's had a reputation for being that school. The one where most of the kids who attended, had parents who were quite wealthy. That simple fact made the kids feel privileged and that they were somehow better than their peers. Elaina had to work two jobs, just to make ends meet. Elaina had made a promise that when it was time for Elle to attend college, she would ensure she was able to. Elaina cleaned a few houses during the week. At night and on the weekend, she worked at Yannie's, one of the local restaurants. She waited tables and would bartend when needed. The hours were crappy, but the tips were good. The bonus was she was able to indulge in her love for seafood without the insane price.

Elle had applied to college to mostly satisfy her mother. Deep down she felt like her mom had missed out on the experience of college life and was trying to live vicariously through her. Elaina had been awarded a full scholarship to SMU, only to get pregnant her sophomore year. The timing never seemed right for her to go back. Especially since she was left to raise Elle on her own. Elaina, didn't have any family to help her except her Aunt Mag. Although Magdalene was not much help, she tried when she could. When Elle was smaller, she would watch her, or you could say Elle would watch her aunt sleep. Elaina never talked about Elle's father. To be honest there were only a few times that Elle even thought about him or wondered what he was like. Elle was close to her mom, and she cherished their bond. Even when she was younger, she asked for a little brother or sister. That never happened. Her mom never really dated anyone more than for a few weeks. She'd always say, "I had my chance at love." That would be the end of the conversation.

Elle was a pretty girl, when she wanted to be. That was just the problem, she never particularly seemed to care about her appearance. She wore glasses, although she had contacts as well, she would only wear those for special occasions. Her everyday style mostly consisted of sweatpants, and oversized t-shirts. Elle's hair was brown, and always pulled up in a ponytail. Elaina often tried to get her to change up her style but it never worked. She had hopes that with her going to college she might change up a bit, but no such luck.

To help with the cost of tuition, Elle was granted work-study. The work assignment she signed up for was to work in the library. Elle loved to read. She was very smart, book smart that is. From a young age, she had a fascination for reading. Elle was excited that on the application for SMU, there was an essay that had to be completed about what novel inspired her most.

"Mom, I'm all packed. You will be happy to know that we can leave on time in the morning."

Elle decided to pack her mom's 2017 candy apple red Dodge Durango with her things early rather than waiting until the last moment. She was walking down the porch steps and tripped headfirst toward the pavement. Luckily, she hit her head on one of her bags full of clothes.

"Not again,"

Elaina heard Elle yelling and rushed to the front door looking out at her daughter sprawled on the pavement.

"I know if I offer my help, you're going to tell me no. You can handle yourself."

Elaina had been a witness to her daughter falling since she began walking. As much as she wished to rescue her baby, she knew she had to resist the urge.

Once she collected herself, Elle proceeded to pack the truck. When she was letting the back hatch down, she slammed her finger in the door. *Why can't I just stay here? I don't want to be the butt of those snobby kids' jokes.* She knew it was no use arguing the fact with her mom.

The next morning came all too early for Elle, but there was no use fighting it. Today was the day, she would have to survive without her mom. As they were making the hour-long drive, Elaina tried to reassure her daughter that she would always be there.

"It's going to be okay, sweetheart. Mommy promises, if you need me, I'm only a call away."

In her mind she hoped that her daughter would finally move away from the shyness stage. Elle was going to be nineteen in a few weeks. It was time for her to spread her wings. Deep down Elaina didn't want her daughter to have the regrets that she did.

Once they arrived on campus, Elle eyes widened. Elaina felt more comfortable about dropping her only child off. Elle jumped out of the truck before her mom came to a complete stop. Of course, being her clumsy self, she scraped her foot on the pavement.

"Ouch Mom. That actually hurt."

Elaina just looked at her child and wryly shook her head.

The rest of the day went by uneventfully. Elaina watched her daughter navigate through getting settled into her room, getting her schedule, and finally checking in to the library to get her work study assignment like a pro. Her little girl was about to be on her own. *She wasn't ready. Elle wasn't ready either. Shake it off Elaina, she will be fine.* Finally, it was time for her to go home and leave her child to fend for herself. After they had dinner with all the other freshmen and their parents, well a third of them, she climbed into her Durango, and drove home in silence. The incoming freshman class had 897 students; she only hoped her daughter wouldn't get lost in the shuffle.

The first few days Elle missed her mom, but she didn't want to call and make her worry. She knew calling would only make things hard for them both. Elle figured she would wait to call her when she had something to tell her. She was settling into her classes well, and she had worked at the library since her second day on campus. Elle was enjoying the time there, if she wasn't doing homework, she was reading. That was her happy place.

On Elle's sixth day of working in the library, a gentleman walked up to her. That was not abnormal. It happened quite often, she sat at the front desk most days to help people find what they needed. This gentleman seemed overdressed to be just standing in the library and he spoke with an accent that she was not familiar with. He inquired if they had any books on Procilla, a country she had never heard of.

By the look on her face, he realized she wasn't familiar with it. He would have liked to know that the country he loved wasn't hidden from the rest of the world.

"Elle, is it? I will be back in a few minutes, that'll give you time to gather the literature that I require."

Elle nodded her head, already using the computer to pull up the country of Procilla. Without looking up at him,

"I will have it for you in a few. Would you like us to call you when they are ready? If so, just jot your number down and we will take care of it."

"No need, I shall return."

He turned on his heel and walked off. *She is an interesting character.* Truth was he had no idea just how interesting.

Elle made quick work of locating all the books that were about Procilla. She was amazed at how many books there was. Just as she was finishing up, the stranger was walking back towards the counter. He perused through the stack and pulled out two of them.

"I would like to check these out."

He pulls out a library card, that had faculty guest on it instead of simply student or faculty, which was what she was accustomed to seeing.

"Sure thing. How long do you need it for?"

Elle noticed the gentleman was looking at her intensely. When he noticed her watching him, he just flashed her a winning smile. The stranger did not answer her question, so she proceeded to tell him the checking out policy.

"You have two weeks from now Sir, if you need the materials for longer you will have to come back in and recheck it out."

"Thank you, it will be returned on Monday. I don't think I will need it any longer than that. By the way my name is Malcom. Thank you for all of your assistance."

Since it was Saturday after her shift at the library, she called her mom and told her she was going to catch the bus home since she had an extra day off from classes on Monday. Elaina fussed a little because Elle didn't call her so she could have picked her up.

"Mom I knew you were probably tired, you worked, today didn't you?"

Elle already knew the answer. *One day, you won't have to work so hard. Things will get better.* Elle felt that there was no way her mom should be working so hard for them to just barely be getting by. Her mom deserved to be happy.

Once Elle had her bags all packed, she caught a cab to the bus station. She had checked out one of the books on Procilla. That was the one thing about her; she had an insatiable thirst for knowledge. She almost missed her stop because she had become so engrossed in the book. It told her all about their history and the pictures were stunning. *Maybe one day I can take Mom there.*

"Mom, I'm home."

Elle called as she unlocked the door and pushed it open, almost falling into the house.

"Come in the living room, baby."

As Elle was turning the corner from the foyer to head into the living room, she saw the back of a man. This was not normal for a man to be in her house alone with her mom. Something must be wrong. At that moment, the man turned around. It was Malcom, the man from the library on campus. *What was he doing here? With her mom?* Elle wanted answers and was about to demand them, but she didn't have a chance to.

"Elle, we have something very important to tell you," her mom offered up. Elaina's face was a little flustered.

"What is it Mom? Why is Malcolm here? How do you know him? This is a little weird, he was just at my school."

Malcolm stepped forward a few inches, moving closer towards her.

"Elle, my apologizes for not being more forthcoming at the library. I just wanted a chance to know you, or well see you just as you. I'm sure everything will make sense in a few moments after your mother and I tell you what is going on."

Malcolm saw the hesitation warring with confusion in Elle's face.

"First of all, baby, it wasn't my intention to be dishonest with you ever. Malcolm is not a stranger, he is actually your father."

Elle's gaze ping-ponged between the two people standing before her.

"What? You have to be kidding me Mom."

"Elle, what your mother is trying to say, and I know this may come as a surprise to you, but hear us out. I am your father. It was my choice because of obligations to my country to not be present in your life. I sent monetary contributions which your mom just told me she put into a trust for you. That will be at your disposal when you turn 21."

Elaina closed the gap between herself and her only child. Malcolm continued,

"Although you won't need it at that time. That is unless you decline what I am about to say."

Elle took a deep breath as he continued. Her mom was holding her hand and pulling her down onto the couch. Malcolm seemed a little more at ease and sat down also.

"Elle my dear, you are actually a princess. I took those

books because I didn't want you to see my picture in them. Procilla is where I am from, I am the King there, therefore that makes you a princess."

He paused to see if she was going to say anything. She did not. The only thing he noticed is her eyes got wide, and she turned to her mom.

"Why didn't you tell me any of this? Not that it would change much, because you are my mom and always will be. But I have a whole dad. Wait...I have a dad who didn't want me."

Elaina couldn't allow Malcolm to take the full blame.

"Elle, it was a mutual choice. Not just one sided. We had to keep you safe. Attempts had been made upon his life and the lives of his family. They simply could not know about you."

Malcolm leaned forward as he began to speak again.

"This is not the way it was meant for you to find out. I meant to come sooner but there was so much going on. Although that doesn't excuse it. The important thing is that I am here now. I must be completely transparent with you. There is an ulterior motive as to my arrival into your life. I am sick, dying from cancer. It can not be treated at this point. They have given me a timeline, and well let's just say, it leaves a lot to be desired. I came here to see if you would come with me to Procilla and claim your rightful place on the throne. I know this is all a shock for you. I can give you a short window of time to decide. Your mother is welcome to be there every step of the way. In fact, I think I'd prefer it."

As he said that he looked over at Elaina and smiled gently.

"Elle, may I have a moment with your mother?"

Elle nodded dazedly and made her way to her room.

CHAPTER TWO

$\mathcal{E}$lle opens the door to her room; her mind is going 100 miles an hour. *How in one moment she goes from being a clumsy young lady whose Mom had to scrape together money for bills to becoming a princess? Not only that, she has a whole dad, that she only has a few months to get to know before he passes away. Getting to know him was contingent upon if she will go to Procilla. Leave school and become a princess.* Who was Elle kidding she would go as long as her mom was going to come along.

"Elle, come here sweetheart."

"Coming Mom."

Elle spoke to her mom in an enthusiastic tone.

"I have decided that I would like to go. I want to know my father at least a little. We can't make up the lost time, but we can enjoy the time he has left."

As she said the last part Elle looked toward her father for reassurance. As if he could read her mind, he smiled at her.

Just then, her father spoke up.

"I know this came about rather suddenly but I want you

to know, I have loved you from the moment your mom told me you existed. We were college kids and we made an amazing young lady from what I gather. I can never express how sorry I am that I wasn't a part of your growing up. With the time we have left I would like to show you how much you mean to me. At the same time, I want you to claim what is rightfully yours. I won't lie to you, if you choose not to accept the crown, it will go to Prince Simon. His family has tried to single handedly ruin our country. I can't let that happen. My parents would roll over in their grave."

Elle couldn't believe that this was happening. She walked over to her mom, when she reached out to grab her hand, she somehow missed and ended up face planting onto the couch.

Malcolm wasn't used to seeing Elle and her uncoordinated behaviors. Elaina smiled to herself her daughter's father would soon find out.

Looking toward Malcolm, Elle said,

"Calling you Dad seems weird to me. Maybe that will change as time goes on. I hope that you can handle that. Or am I supposed to call you, Your Highness? Because truthfully, I cannot do that, unless I have to."

Malcolm shook his head, and walked towards Elle,

"That will come or maybe it won't. I know I didn't give you much time to figure it out. Even if it doesn't that is okay. Malcolm would be fine. The important thing is knowing that you will be coming back home with me. That you will be taking your rightful place as the Princess of Procilla. I wish you could have been treated as royalty your whole life. You deserved that. I will never be able to apologize enough to you or your mom. I thought I was doing what was best. My country meant everything to our family, but it never should have come before you. If I had a chance to do it all over again, I would do it so differently. I know now that both worlds can coexist. I didn't have to make a choice. I am so sorry that I did not figure it out sooner. The other part was that there has always been a hint of danger. Our family as most royals are targets in one form or another. I was trying to navigate through that and run a country. I finally have a handle on it. At least I think I do."

Malcolm was overjoyed that Elle decided that she would go with him. He didn't know exactly why she agreed but he was overjoyed nonetheless. The throne would be saved, and he would get the opportunity to know her.

"Malcolm, my, well our, daughter deserves to get to know you. What can I do to help?"

"Elaina, if you would accompany us to Procilla that would be wonderful. Elle is going to need you now more than ever. There will be lessons in etiquette and the politics of the country."

Looking at Elle, he smiled at his daughter.

"It won't be easy. And for that I apologize ahead of time."

"I know your semester just started, and I hate to disrupt your life, but it is imperative that we begin the training as soon as possible. There is one more thing, now don't freak out on me. You will have to select a husband."

Gagging cough...Elle almost lost a lung. He definitely caught her off guard with that one.

"I'm not ready for marriage. I just learned I have a father, that I am a princess by birthright. Now you want me to pick a husband?"

"You wouldn't have to marry them right away. There is a period of getting to know each other. Your mother and I fell in love, and I would love for you to have a relationship like that."

Elaina spoke up for the first time since Malcolm asked her to come along.

"Malcolm, I would love to come with you and Elle, but there are some things that I would have to get settled here first. I can be there within a week or two tops."

"It's settled, if you agree Elle, we can leave in a few days. That should be time enough to get your school affairs taken care of. So, are we in agreeance that by Monday we can leave?"

Elle shook her head in agreeance.

Malcolm excused himself for the evening. He turned as he opened the front door and mentioned.

"I will take the liberty of handling the University, and your academic affairs. There won't be any negative remarks as if you dropped out. It will be as if you never were enrolled. Once things settle down at home, you can take some classes if you want and get your degree. I wouldn't dream of taking that from you."

Malcolm paused for a moment as he contemplated reaching out for a hug, but he remained poised and extended his hand. Elle surprised him and moved in for a hug. He exhaled, maybe this would not be so bad after all.

The next few days went by in a blur. Elle spent most of her time trying to get her things brought back home from campus. The rest of the time she spent packing and enjoying spending some quality time with her mom. Being an hour away from Elaina wasn't so bad, but when it came to be living over 23 hours away that was major. She hadn't been farther than 5 hours from her mom her entire life.

Elle was having second thoughts about going to a foreign country with a man she didn't know. Elle wished she had more time to get to know him with the buffer of her mom being around. That way she would feel more comfortable.

Monday arrived all too soon. Malcolm had a car waiting outside of the house at 8 am sharp. Elaina was torn between letting her daughter go and keeping her all to herself. *She doesn't need that life. We can enjoy the one that we have.* Elaina knew that wasn't okay for her to think nor act like that. She promised her daughter she would be there in a week or so.

"Mommy, I'm not sure if I want to really go."

"Baby, don't start this. You already told your father that you would be on that plane, or jet."

"Mom, I don't know him. What if the people don't like me?"

"There will always be what if's no matter the scenario. I know your father would never do anything to harm you or allow you to be put into any danger. I trust him with my own life."

At that moment, Elaina reached and pulled her daughter into a long hug that seemed to have lasted an eternity. Once they let go, it seemed all too short.

The moment was interrupted further by a knock at the door.

Elle went and opened the door to see a middle age gentleman standing there. He had dark hair with traces of salt and pepper. The man was dressed in a suit that was obviously tailored just for him.

"Good Morning Your Highness, my name is Frank, I will be your driver for today. I believe we have an 10 am flight departure time. Do you have bags that need to be put into the car?"

It took Elle a moment to realize he was indeed speaking to her, she was going to have to get used to the whole 'Your Highness,' thing.

"Yes sir. I do have a few bags. Somehow I don't think my clothes will be appropriate for where we are going."

"Your father will be meeting us at the airport. Once we arrive at our destination, I believe he said you would be going shopping. So, Your Highness that works out perfectly. We should arrive back in Procilla, Tuesday morning, or mid-day if there aren't any delays. The country is eagerly awaiting your arrival."

Elle grabbed her mother for another long hug. Elaina knew it was the right thing to do for her daughter to embrace her birthright.

"Come on baby, let's get your things in the car. Your new life awaits. You will be amazing."

Elle was walking to the car with her backpack with most of her important things and tripped when she was reaching for the door to the car.

Elaina could only chuckle and shake her head. Elle was stepping into her new role as only she could, tumbling head over heels.

CHAPTER THREE

*E*lle and Frank spoke very little during the flight. She asked him questions about her father. Frank told her that he was employed by the royal family for many years. He had watched her father grow up and he eventually assumed control of the throne.

"I think your father would be better equipped to answer your questions. He was excited that he was coming to see you."

"How do you know that? He never tried before."

"Believe me, if he wasn't loyal to his country, you and your mom would have been with him. If she would have had him. He always felt he missed his chance with you both. But again, Your Highness, he is better suited to answer any of your questions. He may act intimidating but don't fall for it. Your father just doesn't know how to express his emotions very well. He hasn't ever had to. Take it easy on him."

Elle decided to take the words Frank said and marinate on them as she took a nap. She thought her father was exaggerating, but no such luck. He didn't just abandon she and her mom. Elle had read stories of how kings sometimes had to make hard sacrifices and often lost the ones they loved. Elle had thought Malcolm was doing some major overselling of his importance and his role, as well as about her mom.

Frank put a movie on the drop-down projector screen. Elle laid back and finally dozed off. She woke up still a few hours out, but only long enough to use the bathroom. Elle was exhausted, and this flight seemed to do the trick for her to get some rest.

Elle's mind began going into overdrive at the thoughts of what was awaiting her when they arrived at her new home. Procilla, her new home to be. It still didn't seem plausible when she spoke out loud that she was royalty. All little girls dream about this kind of thing when growing up, but it was now her reality. She wasn't ready.

The plane shook. She hadn't experienced turbulence before, but she knew she didn't like it. It happened when she was walking back to her seat from the restroom. Of course, being her natural self, she fell forward. Frank disconnected his seatbelt and went to assist her off the floor. Elle laughed so hard tears began to stream down her face. Wait until her mom finds out that she couldn't even make it a day without tripping.

"Ma'am, are you alright?"

"Yes, Frank and thank you for assisting me to my feet."

Frank would eventually learn just as everyone else, that the floor no matter which one, was her nemesis. Elle continued laughing to herself.

"Ms. Elle we are approaching Procilla. If you look out the window, you can see how beautiful she is."

Frank began briefing her as to what she could expect upon their landing. Elle blocked out most of what he said except the part about the tour.

As the plane started making its descent into Procilla, she began getting more and more nervous by the second. Looking out the window there were people everywhere. This was one of those things Frank tried to warn her about. Frank saw her anxious expression and looked out the window.

"Ms. Elle, the people are eager to get a look at their future Queen. Up until recently, not many knew of your existence. Some still believe it is just a ruse put on by your father to keep the throne away from Prince Simon and his family. Your father has a lot riding on this. He wants you to want this life, therefore it will be better for you. King Malcolm loves his country and he truly wants you to love it too."

After they landed and they disembarked the plane, Elle was whisked off into a darkly tinted limousine. It all happened so quickly that none of the tabloid reporters were able to get a picture snapped. Frank was happy about that fact. He remembered a time when there was a photo of the Queen that had been photoshopped in a compromising position. Frank remembered that time all too well. The reporters used his picture alongside the Queen's. It took a year or so for that to finally get erased. The Queen and King would often joke about it, Frank saw no humor in it at all. His respect for the Crown weighed more than most.

As they pulled up to the castle, Elle had to catch her breath. She knew her father lived in a castle, but not like a fairy tale castle. Malcolm was standing on the top stair waiting for her to arrive. With him, was about 20 members of the castle's staff.

"Hello Elle. How was your trip? I truly hope Frank didn't bore you to death."

Elle's mouth was just as wide as her eyes in amazement. Other than in fairy tale stories, and the Queen's home in

England, she had never seen a castle. She truly didn't know what to expect at all. It wasn't this. This was to be her new home. This castle in her mind faired well compared to the Queen's.

Malcolm reached for her hand and began ushering her inside. What was normal for him, he began to think would be too overwhelming for his daughter.

"Are you ready for your tour or would you like to freshen up a bit first?"

"Do I have time to freshen up and maybe take a quick nap? I am feeling a little lightheaded and nauseous."

"Of course, there is plenty of time. Glenda, can you show my daughter where her room is located and make sure she has what she needs please."

"Right away, Your Majesty."

Turning to Elle, she says, "Right this way ma'am. Oscar will grab your bags and bring them to your room."

The whole having someone waiting on her was something she knew she would have to get used to. Because it has always been just Elle and her mom, she became self-sufficient at an early age. She would often make Elaina breakfast and or dinner. Those were the times she knew she would miss the most right now. As her mind drifted to her mom and being alone. She knew she wasn't resting properly or eating properly. Elle made up her mind she would call her later that night.

Elle was lost in thought as they climbed the staircase that seemed to wind forever. Once they reached the top of the staircase, Glenda guided her towards the doorway to the right.

"The King's room is just on the other side of the hall. Although it seems these days, he is rarely in there."

Of course, his door would be a royal blue in color. Her

father looked strong and bold not like he was easily swayed in his convictions. There were a few others in beautiful deep colors of purple, red and green. The door she was ushered inside of was purple. Which worked out great since that was her favorite color. Elle's eyes widened as she stepped into the room. The inside of the room was ginormous. It appeared to be larger than her and her mom's apartment. Glenda smiled to herself.

"Ma'am, do you approve?"

Elle could only shake her head in agreement.

"This is amazing. It is too big though for just little ol' me. Maybe when my mom arrives, she will stay in here too."

"No ma'am, your mother will be in the "Emerald Suite." It is being prepared for her as we speak."

Glenda began showing Elle around the room. There was a huge walk in closet, that was filled with clothes, there was a separate closet that was filled with beautiful gowns in all colors and styles. Elle found herself feeling anxious and overwhelmed.

"Ms. Glenda, I would just like to lie down for a bit. My mind can't comprehend all this right now. This place is gorgeous."

"Of course, ma'am. And it is just Glenda please. How long would you like to rest? I can wake you up if you like."

"Maybe just an hour or two tops. I know Father is eager for me to take the tour."

"As you wish ma'am. I will leave you now. Have a nice rest."

Just as Glenda was closing the door, there was a loud thud. Pushing the door back open, she saw Elle on the floor with one of her bags on top of her. Elle was laughing uncontrollably.

"I'm okay." she said in between giggles. "I promise I'm okay. This happens all the time."

Glenda only shook her head and pulled the door closed. Thinking to herself, *the castle is going to be different now.* Glenda had been in the service of the royal family since she was twelve. There had never been a young adult royal, besides King Malcolm. Smiling to herself, "I hope the staff can handle her."

Elle gathered herself up off the floor and jumped onto the bed. Her body was exhausted from the flight, but her mind was all over the place. She closed her eyes and sleep found her fast. Elle dreamt of her mom and she dreamt of being a royal. Just as quickly as she had drifted off, she woke up in a panic. It took her a moment to realize she wasn't home anymore. After laying there for a bit longer, Elle realized she wasn't going back to sleep just yet. Elle gathered her toiletries and headed for the en suite to freshen up.

After she had showered and put on some fresh clothing, she went down the long winding staircase. Glenda was waiting at the bottom, almost as if she knew she was coming down. As if reading her mind,

"Yes ma'am, I heard the shower running. Your room is above mine. It was planned that way since I am your maid and personal assistant after all. I knew it was only a matter of time before you came down. I wanted to be ready to take you on your tour. Your father will join us midway through."

The tour began with the first level of the castle and moved up the staircase. The tour took over 2 hours. Elle knew she hadn't been to all the nooks and crannies, but it was overwhelming. She was glad when they made their way back down the winding staircase to meet up with her father.

King Malcolm reached for her hand and guided her away from Glenda.

"Thank you, Glenda I have it from here. I think it is about time for me to spend some time with my beautiful daughter."

Elle was not used to those words at all. Her cheeks turned red as crimson. Of course, her mom called her beautiful at times, but it still wasn't something she was used to. She liked hearing it from him. Growing up she never really missed out on having a father too much, but she imagined it would have been great to hear that from him as a child who was as awkward as she was.

"I apologize the tour was supposed to be brief, but we get rather excited about our home and the grounds."

Elle was enjoying the tour so far. They were turning to go toward the garden and her father stopped abruptly. She could tell he had begun to relax around her. Elle instantly looked in the direction of a handsome man. His hair was jet black; his eyes were slate blue. The grey overrode the blue. This guy's smile was gorgeous. Elle regained control of herself, her father's sudden change in demeanor must mean he is not a friend.

"Prince Simon how are you doing these days? Haven't seen you sneaking about as of late."

"Hello, Your Majesty, no sneaking around here. Just familiarizing myself with the grounds. This will after all be my home one day."

Under his breath Malcolm let out a sigh.

As he was talking, he cut his eyes at Elle, looking her up and down. He didn't even try to hide it.

"I beg your pardon, my name is Simon, and you are?"

Elle looked at her father as he answered for her.

"This is Princess Elle, my daughter, and soon to be Queen of Procilla. Elle, this young chap is Prince Simon, his family has some delusion about getting the crown. Now that you are here, that puts an end to that notion, right Simon?"

"It is a pleasure to meet you Princess." Simon extended his hand to Elle. Hesitantly she accepted it. After all her family's enemies must be hers as well. Right?

"To be fair Your Majesty, whatever my family has done towards the crown has nothing to do with me. I have nothing but the utmost respect for you and the crown, and always have."

"Come to think of it, Simon, you are correct. I will have to remember that. I wish you a good day. I must continue showing my daughter the grounds. You understand, don't you?"

"Of course, Your Majesty, Princess."

Taking Elle by the arm, Malcolm guides her to the long walkway lined with roses. The two continued on their tour. Elle was determined not to ask her father about Simon. She was a little relieved when he finally brought him up after a few moments of silence.

"Elle, as you know, I told you there was someone who wanted to take over the throne in the event of my death. Simon's family seems to feel very strongly about it. They have eluded to the fact that they were cheated out of it many years ago. I have spent countless hours researching it myself, I can't find any wrongdoing to justify their behavior. That doesn't mean it didn't happen. There is just no record of it. Your grandfather, was born into the monarchy as was I."

Malcolm sighed at the memory of his father, King Jonathan. He regretted that Elle would never know his parents. That was one thing he had also felt disheartened about. They would have loved her. Queen Re'gine always wanted a daughter and would have surely doted on her granddaughter.

Snapping himself out of it. Malcolm smiled at his daughter. She had his mother's eyes. In a way this reassured him that he was making the right decision. It was time that his daughter was home where she belonged.

The two continued their walk ending up deep in the depths of the massive garden. This wasn't the typical garden Elle was used to seeing. This garden had only roses. There were so many rose bushes but what made them more special was that there were different colors. The colors ranged from purple to pink, black, and gold. Elle had never seen so many beautiful colors in her life. Malcolm explained the significance of the colors. He told her he had sent her mom a blue one after he left to come back home to symbolize a secret. Malcolm told her; this color was very rare to find. His mother had a love for roses, so she asked King Jonathan for this one thing, a garden of every color rose someone had seen. He loved her so much he made it happen. Malcolm saw to it that it was kept up as his parents aged. He would take his mother one of each color every morning at breakfast time.

Having lost track of time, Malcolm tells Elle they need to head back toward the house. It would be time to eat soon. Elle was wide eyed and in awe of the grounds and the palace. She thought about how fun it would have been growing up there. *How much stuff would have been broken due to my clumsiness?*

"Elle, you should go get cleaned up and let's meet in the grand-dining room in about 30 minutes?" Her father said looking at his watch.

"Yes Sir, I will be right back down."

Elle had been enjoying her day so far, it was a little overwhelming, but she was enjoying spending time with her father. There was only one thing missing so far, her mom. Elle did not want to worry Malcolm that she was homesick already, she had to be strong for him. As a Princess she could not show signs of being weak. That is when people would try you and the next thing you know, you are booted from your throne. At least that is how it happened in the movies.

Over dinner Elle and Malcolm discussed some of the things that were to come. Unfortunately for Elle there wasn't a lot of time, but she was to choose a prince to marry.

"In the morning my dear you will begin your history training. Glenda will be with you most of the time going forward. She will set your appointments, keep track of your correspondence, among other things. There is one thing I must tell you. As a way of allowing our people to get to know you and fall in love with you, the whole process will be televised." He immediately saw the look on her face, almost one of abject horror. "Don't fret, it will be fine, I promise you. You will have to sign a waiver for the show. That is if you consent. We got the idea from America's *"The Bachelor"*. Glenda was trying to find a way to make it beneficial for the country as well as giving you the best chance to find a suitable husband without too much awkwardness."

Malcolm smiled as he said it. Only on national tv would it be less awkward for his daughter to find a husband and impress a whole country.

Elle had a lot to take in. After dinner she excused herself to go upstairs to her room. She knew she had a lot of work ahead of her. Elle just wanted to shower and get some sleep. As bad as she wanted to hear her mom's voice reassuring her that all was going to be okay, she was too exhausted to call.

CHAPTER FOUR

*O*ver the next few weeks, Elle's days had been filled with studying the history of Procilla. She learned that her family had been in control for three generations and that she would be the fourth. Knowing this made her nervous. She didn't want to mess this up. Nor did she want to be the reason the monarchy fell. Elle also had a front seat to witness the love her father has for his country and their people. They have had reporters all around the palace taking photos of her and her father. King Malcolm handled it all with class. He held a press conference every week.

"Pretty soon you will see just how amazing my daughter is. She is getting acclimated to our beautiful country. Trust me you will love her as I do. I will continue letting you all know that this is happening. She is going to make her a new life here and you guys are indeed the lucky ones."

He tried his best to reassure them that the monarchy was safe. Each week a new reporter was swearing she was a scandal in the making. Malcolm had promised himself and Elle that he would take care of all of that idle chatter. All she had to do was take her time and soak up all the knowledge that she could. Malcolm was proud of the progress that she had made thus far. Their dinners were filled with quizzes every evening. She was passing them with no problem. He knew she was meant to be here. She would be great for the country. Malcolm loved how she looked at life. Even though her mom and she may have struggled a little she didn't just see the ugly in the world.

Elaina was finally coming to visit. Elle was super excited; at breakfast she barely ate. She couldn't stop talking about Elaina. Malcolm knew it was hard for her not to have her mom with her. Truthfully, he missed Elaina as well. They always had a connection, and the years didn't change that. Malcolm insisted that he would pick Elaina up himself from the airport.

"Sir, you do want me to drive though right?" Frank asked hesitantly.

Malcolm nodded in reply. It was hard for him to contain his excitement. He had always wanted Elaina to come to Procilla, but she was adamant about that not happening. 19 years later and it was finally happening. Malcolm was excited to see if she would fall in love with Procilla the way he did many years ago. It may be too late for them but, he knew his daughter would need her mother to help her along in running the country.

Glenda had been preparing Elle for what would happen on the show. Elle felt a little funny about getting to know guys, especially on TV. The closest she had come to dating anyone was her prom date. Ryan was her chem lab partner and he didn't want to go to prom. Elle kindly reminded him of the pact they made in the 9th grade. So, prom it was. They had a nice time but afterwards they agreed it was weird. The first and last date between she and Ryan came with pictures that her mom loved. That in itself made it worthwhile for Elle to go to prom.

Elle was a little disappointed that she wasn't going to be able to meet her mother at the airport, but Glenda just wouldn't ease up. The film crew started showing up and setting things up early that morning. It was all a little over-whelming to Elle, but she tried to remain calm.

"Your Highness, you will be introduced to six bachelors this evening. They have all been vetted. A few of them are in line to a crown themselves. The line is quite long, but they are there nonetheless."

Glenda tried to joke, but Elle was not in the joking mood.

"All of them are royalty so they would know what is expected of them as your suitor. That is if they happened to be chosen. They have been groomed from an early age to take a crown or assist in the responsibility of becoming a ruler."

Glenda began rattling off all the names of the young men, but the one that stuck out was that of Simon. Surely, she couldn't mean the same Simon who was already trying to lay claim to the throne. Glenda saw the look on her face and shook her head yes.

"Yes, the same one. Now, please focus your Highness. This is going to happen, and it is going to happen quickly. Your father wants to ensure you are well prepared to accept the crown. In order to do that you have to marry."

An hour or so later, the guys began coming into the house, and were shown where to go. Elle was on the staircase looking down at them as they entered. She smiled to herself, they were all quite handsome in their own way. Maybe this would be fun after all.

Glenda ushered her up the stairs so that she could get ready. Upon entering her room, the telephone was ringing.

Elle's face lit up when she answered it and it was Elaina on the other end.

"Mom! It is so good to hear your voice and to know I will see you soon. Wait, you aren't calling to tell me you are delayed, are you?"

Elaina assured her she wouldn't miss being there for the taping. She explained that she and Malcolm would be along shortly.

Glenda was busying herself with pulling out a chic emerald green pantsuit with some gold heels for Elle to get changed into as soon as she hung up the phone with her mom.

"Come Your Highness, we must hurry and get your hair and makeup done, and we are running out of time."

Elle was trying to stay focused on the endgame, but her nerves began to get the best of her. She felt her breathing start to become erratic. Without warning her heart began to race. Elle felt as if the world was coming to an end in mere moments. Glenda looked over at Elle just in time to rush to her side to extend her arms to catch her before she hit the floor.

"Your Highness, are you okay?" Glenda hated asking her that question. She knew all too well that this was very over-whelming for a young lady of only nineteen years of age. Going on tv and showing the world the inner workings of your life couldn't be easy.

Glenda assisted Elle to the bed so she could lay down for a bit. After doing so, she went to the bathroom and got a cold cloth to wipe Elle's forehead. Elle's eyes started fluttering slowly at first. Slowly she opened her eyes. "This isn't starting off well, huh?"

"Your Highness, would you like me to postpone this meeting?"

Shaking her head, no, "It will happen either way. No need to prolong it. What if something happened to my father? I must be ready to assume the throne. Can you give me a few minutes to get myself together? I will get dressed and then call you back so we can finish up with hair and makeup. I assure you I will be fine. I have to be."

Glenda stopped fussing over her long enough to get herself together and left Elle to get dressed. She worried that this was all a bit much. Even for this high-spirited, yet shy girl.

Once Glenda left the room, Elle stood up steadying herself before she went and took a quick shower. She thought the cool water would do her some good. Knowing she was in jeopardy of getting behind schedule Elle got dressed quickly. When she was done, she called for Glenda.

She hurried in with Elaina on her heels.

"Momma, you made it?"

"Of course, my love. We must hurry up; the males are getting restless and very fidgety. They are quite handsome, I might add.'

About an hour later, Elle was making her way down the staircase to meet her suitors. The camera was on her every move. Her entrance was done in typical fashion, she stumbled missing the last step. Luckily, she didn't fall. If she had, she would have been in good hands, Simon was by her side in a flash. Elle smiled up at him, he smiled back.

As John, the emcee of the show told the people watching a little of Elle's history, the camera paned from her to the guys. They all looked nervous that is except Simon. There was something almost cocky like in his demeanor. Perhaps it was just confidence.

John announced the guys. As he did, they each stepped forward so Elle could get a good look at them. Today was just to introduce everyone and have dinner together. Each of the guys would have time to tell Elle about themselves, more than the short little blurb the announcer had said. Then they would have the opportunity to tell her where they would go on their individual dates.

As they moved into the dining hall, Elle was seated first, then the men. The food was brought out moments later. Some of Elle's favorite foods were anything involving seafood, so that was the theme of their dinner. It would be important that they had similar taste. The waitstaff brought out some lobster bisque soup. When Sir Quincy wrinkled his nose up. Elle spoke up to inquire if he was okay.

"Your Highness, I beg your pardon, but I am a vegetarian. May I have a salad instead?"

Glenda was on it, and a salad was immediately brought out.

Throughout the rest of the meal, it seemed as if Elle was doing more acting instead of truly eating her meal. The lobster looked amazing. If only she could focus on it, but she was trying to get through this. She was asking questions of each of the gentleman. Elle noticed Nigel's face was bright red. He was being a good sport about it all, but he was having an allergic reaction. Nigel refused to leave. Glenda brought him some Benadryl. He thanked her profusely. Something told him to bring his EpiPen.

Being the overprotective dad, Malcolm insisted that the security team would accompany them on all dates outside of the palace. He didn't trust everyone and their intentions. While the young men were waiting for Elle to join them downstairs, Glenda had them all pull numbers. The number they pulled would be the order that they would go on their date. After the dates and times were set. The gentlemen all excused themselves. It had been a long day for the Princess.

She was beyond exhausted, and glad to be able to finally breathe. And where was her mother? She only had a moment with her earlier before the show started taping. Thankfully, she had a couple of days to rest up before the dates were due to begin.

CHAPTER FIVE

Over the next few days, Elle filled her mom in on all that was happening. Elaina told Elle that she would be there with her for a while. This made Elle extremely happy. She hated that Elle had to go through this without her. As her mother, Elaina wanted to ensure that she could be there for her daughter in every way she could – through the good times and the bad. Elaina hadn't been a perfect parent. She knew that. And she wanted to rectify the situation to the best of her abilities.

Malcolm was beyond thrilled that Elaina was joining them. He was having a few bad days and it was getting harder to mask them from Elle. Every now and then, he was tempted to finally tell Elle the truth, to unburden himself, but every time, he stopped himself from doing just that. He didn't want to burden her with things she didn't need to hear right now. Eventually, he knew he would need to tell her that he was worried he wouldn't have long to spend with her, that he would leave her unprepared to rule the country. But not right now. Instead, Malcolm managed to keep a smile upon his face. Besides, it was easier to deal with the bad days knowing that Elle was there to take the reins. The cancer was not responding to the treatments currently. He was due to see a specialist soon enough and perhaps that would prolong his days some.

Elle was beginning to get used to the cameras being around. It hadn't been easy, and she wouldn't exactly say she liked the current predicament she found herself in, but she was growing more accustomed to it. Most of her nervousness had subsided. Having her mom there helped tremendously. It made her feel more at ease. If anything, her mother grounded her, kept her in check, reminded her that she was still the same person she always was before all of this.

The dates were to begin today. She felt she was ready, besides what could go wrong? She had prepared as much as she could, and she had every intention of seeing them through no matter what.

However, Elle also knew that there was a possibility that anything could happen. She didn't want to be the girl who was constantly in denial. Right now, she had a lucky hand and she didn't want to test it.

One morning, Elaina stopped by Elle's room, and gently knocked on the door.

Elle smiled after receiving her mother, and stepped to the side so Elaina could come in.

"Hello, my darling," Elaina said, giving her daughter a kiss on the cheek. "And where's Malcolm?"

"Getting ready." Elle smiled, following her mother into the sitting area. "You okay?"

"I wanted to know if you'd like to go shopping today," she said. "I know you have some very important dates and I wanted to see if there was anything, I could get you to make sure you're ready."

"That's nice of you," Malcolm said as he tied his tie entering the room, "But the outfits have already been purchased and tailored to Elle's exact size. There's nothing that you need to worry about."

Elle saw a flicker of disappointment in her mother's eyes.

"Well," Elaina said through a sigh. "Okay. If you're sure. I just want to be included as much as possible This is the kind of stuff, we mothers want to do with our daughters, you know. I just." She hesitated, sucking in a breath. "I just don't want to miss the important parts." She took Elle's hand in hers. "I know my baby has anxiety issues when she has to behave a certain way or look a certain way. I just want to make sure I'm here for you."

"Oh, Mama, you are here for me," Elle said as she gave her mother a quick hug.

"She's been doing splendidly, Elaina" he assured her. He finally gave up on his tie and Elle stepped forward, her fingers moving seamlessly across the silk.

"Hmm."

"I promise, Mama, if I need you, I know how to reach you." Elle looked over her shoulder at Elaina. "Trust me, even when I get uncomfortable, I take your advice and smile through it."

"She does," Malcolm said when Elle finished. "It's amazing to see. I'm honored to be part of it." He smiled. "I only wished I could spend more time with her."

"Well, okay." Elaina shifted her weight. "I would like to talk to my daughter before you leave for your first date if you don't mind?" She arched a brow.

He held up his hands. "Not at all," he said. "I'll leave you to it."

After he disappeared back into his bedroom, Elaina turned to her daughter. "You can do this, baby," she said. "But know you can always change your mind. That doesn't make you flighty, you hear me? It makes you brave."

"I know, Mama. Thank you."

After Elaina left, Ella took a seat on the couch and waited. She couldn't believe what she was about to embark on. How lucky of Simon to have pulled the number 1. She shook her head, forcing herself to her feet. There were only a few minutes before their date, and she wanted to make sure she was ready. This wasn't a moment that would come again.

Simon could not wait to meet up with Elle again. He planned to take her on a carriage ride and end up at a bistro in the plaza. Simon's intention was to share Procilla' s history as well as one of her greatest treasures, her finest cuisine, Lobster Gnocchi. This was the ultimate summer pasta. Simon got a feeling that Elle didn't have a chance to actually enjoy her food from the other night. He wanted her to feel at home and be able to enjoy the culture and all that Procilla had to offer.

Simon was a little annoyed that the security detail was following them around, but he felt he could work his magic anyway. He wanted to win her over.

The moment Elle saw Simon, her breath disappeared. He looked absolutely beautiful in his white collared shirt and his charcoal slacks tailored for his body "Good morning Your Highness." She barely got the words out.

"I'm sorry about the security," he said, gallantly offering her his arm. "I can't really lose them, even though I'd like nothing more than to be alone with you." He flashed her a cheeky grin.

"I understand," she said, taking his arm. "So, you're lucky number one?"

"I do feel pretty lucky right now, if I am just being honest." Simon flashed a grin at Elle. Unbeknownst to Elle, Simon had taken an interest in her. He wanted more than anything to be the one she chose to be by her side. Elle wasn't just a ticket to the throne, but she had captured a piece of his heart from their very first meeting. He didn't want to tell her just yet, however. He had seen how bitter his mother and father were and he wanted to ensure he wasn't locked into a relationship like that. If their attitude had taught him anything, it was to be careful who you trusted, but to be open to trusting someone.

As they began their carriage ride, Simon began pointing out historical landmarks. He pointed out the library where her grandmother used to go weekly to read to the children. They passed the hospital, and he told her that once a month she would go to the pediatric floor and to the sick babies who needed some one on one time, she would hold them and sing to them.

"The Queen sounds like she was an amazing woman," Elle murmured, her eyes filled with wonder at hearing so many of the stories. "It's obvious she cared about her people."

Simon could see the uncertainty in her eyes. "Don't worry," he said, placing his hand over hers. "You will find your place, and everyone will love you for being you. It's not a competition you know."

But it was, in a way. He needed to remember that. And

telling Elle it wasn't was belittling what she was going through, which was the last thing he wanted to do.

Elle looked over at Simon, just as he was telling her that they had arrived at their destination.

Simon had wanted to have the restaurant all to themselves, but Malcolm wouldn't hear of it. As much as Malcolm loved Elle, he didn't want to shut down the restaurant for a date.

"If she is to be Queen, she will be Queen to all her people," Simon had insisted after Malcolm had returned from Elle's room after meeting with Elle's mother. "She will not hide from them. Elle must get to know them, and them her."

This was something Malcom would not bend on.

"Are you sure you're up for this?" Simon asked tentatively. "We can always go somewhere else, just the two of us."

"No, we should do this." Simon noticed Elle's jaw flex, but instead of being wary, it seemed determined. Formidable. She turned and locked eyes with him. "These are your people. They're important to you, which makes them important to me."

He grinned. "Let's do this."

Elle came out of the restaurant, rubbing her full stomach. "Probably shouldn't do that," Simon said, a teasing glint in his eyes. He nodded to the paparazzi. "They'll think we somehow produced an heir already."

She laughed. "I'm sorry," she said. "That was just the best meal I have had in a while."

"I'm glad." He took her hand in his, bringing her fingers up so he could brush a kiss against them. His eyes flashed, darkening as he looked at her.

Something twisted in Elle's belly, heat flared through her and she had to look away.

He was the most attractive person she had ever laid eyes upon. It was only natural of her to desire him. And yet, she didn't want to rush into things. She wanted to slow down. She wanted to get to know him better.

After their date, Simon took Elle back to her room. Thankfully, her mother had left so she was alone.

"I had a lovely time with you this evening," he said in a low voice. It crawled up her skin, tempting her. He leaned in and placed a gentle kiss on her lips.

A small whimper left her mouth and she placed her hand over her lips, trying to contain herself.

His eyes only darkened, as though he knew exactly what she meant, exactly what she wanted. He turned and left her alone. Unfortunately for her, she knew she would not be getting any sleep tonight.

CHAPTER SIX

*S*he looked around the room. It was colder than she expected it to be. Where she was exactly, she didn't quite know. The room was unfamiliar to her. A gentle breeze tickling her locks of hair indicated a window was open somewhere. She wrapped her arms around her body. Glancing down, she realized she had on the same dress from her first date with Simon.

She reached around her so she could grab the zipper in her fingers.

"Wait."

The command was soft, gentle.

She jumped, not expecting anyone.

"I'll help you."

The familiar voice wrapped around her like a warm blanket and a shudder ripped down her spine.

She shouldn't be here. The competition's rules were clear. She couldn't have any interaction that wasn't scheduled. And yet, stepping away, out of this room – she realized it belonged to him – was like stepping out of quicksand – impossible.

He moved around her until he was just behind Elle's frame. Her knees grew weak. Somehow, her body knew where he was even though she still couldn't see him.

"I'm going to touch you," he said.

She nodded once. Hopefully he could understand that she was giving him her consent, but she appreciated the fact that he wasn't assuming that he had the right to do so, despite the fact that she was in this competition.

One hand suddenly cupped her waist while the other took the zipper in his hands and slowly began to tug downward. The cool air pinched her skin, causing goosebumps to erupt all over her body. She hissed in a breath as the top of her dress began to fall forward. Her breasts spilled out, nipples hardening. She wanted so badly to reach up and cover herself, but she found she couldn't move.

Slowly, so slowly, the dress tumbled to the floor, surrounding her in a big halo of magenta. She was left in nothing more than silky black underwear, underwear she picked out, underwear she wasn't expecting anyone to see. It made her feel confident, though, and in a competition like this one, she needed all the confidence she could get.

He still stood behind her. Even though he wasn't touching her, she could feel him, could feel his presence. And she wanted him to break that barrier, to push through it and tantalize her skin with the caress of his own. She wanted to feel him. She wanted –

She swallowed.

She wanted what she shouldn't want.

She sighed.

"Thank you." She tilted her head to the side. She didn't want to turn completely, not when her breasts were bare. Not when she was so exposed, so vulnerable.

"Is there anything else I can help you with?" His voice was so close to her. How had he gotten so close without her noticing? Was

she so focused on what could have happened that she didn't realize what was happening?

Without warning, one index finger slid through the hook of her panties and he began to tug them down. She swallowed, closing her eyes. Her mind and body warred within herself. She wanted to push him away. She'd never done this before. She wanted her first time to be special, and the last thing she wanted was something hanging between them. In their case, she didn't want him to assume that just because there was a competition between them didn't mean she was using sex to get an advantage.

But then the question was, did she want this? And if she did, why shouldn't she have it? She and Simon were two consenting adults. No one had to know what happened between them. It was no one's business.

And what if Simon uses you and still doesn't pick you?

The case could be made that she was using him as well, couldn't it? She wanted him to make her feel good. She wanted him to please her in a way no one else had before. There was nothing wrong with that, was there?

"Simon," she breathed out.

He pulled harder, but not enough to destroy her underwear. At least he had the frame of mind to be gentle. As much as she wanted to give into her inhibitions and be ferocious, she couldn't. She was still hesitant, maybe even a little scared. But she knew she didn't want him to stop.

"Yes."

Slowly, so slowly, he pulled her underwear down until it was a small pool by her ankles. Simon took her calves in his hands and gently pushed them apart. He spread her legs just a little bit so he had better access to her mound.

Elle swallowed, but her throat was still dry. Inside, she was shaking. But she couldn't push him away.

"I..." She let her voice trail off. She opened her eyes.

What did she want? Did she want him to stop? Why would she, when his hands felt so good on her body – and that was only her ankles. How good would it feel when he traced her curves, when he cupped her ass, when he nibbled her ear.

The thought of him assaulting her body in such a way caused a whimper to fall off her lips. Her head rolled back, a sigh flew out of her nose, and her body knew the answer to her dilemma before her mind was able to catch up.

"Don't stop."

The words were more confident than I actually felt.

I turned around despite his hands on my thighs. I wanted to see him, I wanted to see his eyes. He looked up at me, his eyes a darker shade of blue. I could see desire ripple in his irises the same way I used to skip pebbles on the nearby lake. I bit my bottom lip, consumed by the gentle breeze and his hungry eyes.

I sucked in a breath.

He took hold of her jaw and tilted her head so he could kiss her again. It was slow and tantalizing. Every inch of her felt that kiss from the tips of her toes to the crown of her head. She buzzed with energy, with feeling that connection with another human being, in a way she never had before. When he tilted her head back to deepen the kiss, she opened her mouth, willing to welcome him in whatever capacity he wanted to have her.

She let out a moan and then pulled away, pressing her lips together. Her cheeks flamed in response to her behavior. She shouldn't have done that. Royalty didn't do stuff like that.

"Don't," he told her. She nodded her head, acknowledging her error. "No." He tilted her head up so she could look at him. "I want to hear you. Don't hide yourself from me, whatever they are."

Elle sucked in a breath and rolled her shoulders back. He kissed her again and then again. His hands found her hips, his thumb tracing slow, methodical circles on each of her hips. She let him gently lead her to his bedroom, to his bed. He eased her down on the sheets and slowly spread her legs open. She tensed, unsure if she was ready to give herself to him just yet.

"We can stop," he said. "I just don't want you to be afraid. I promise to make you feel good."

"I just," she breathed out as he began to lower his head to her mound. "I've never –"

Before she could finish the sentence, his mouth was on her. She hissed, unsure of what to feel.

"Don't think so much," he murmured, pulling away from her warmth for the briefest of moments. "Just roll with it."

She laughed despite herself. The last thing she would have assumed to hear in this atmosphere was something so... casual.

It wasn't long before she felt the buildup. She had never felt it before, how it started off slowly, almost unnoticeable. Then, it grew and grew, almost like an earthquake that started out as a mere tremor. Her entire body was suddenly bewitched by it, suddenly and completely contained. When she climaxed, he held her firmly to him so she could not move, so she could experience all that was offered.

When he finished, he picked his head up. "Are you all right?" he asked.

She nodded shyly. Her lips were unable to frown. She couldn't quite explain it. Somehow, she was unable to do anything but smile.

He grinned back at her and her heart skipped a beat.

He crawled over her; his broad shoulders hunched by his ears. He looked like a hungry lion and she could not help but feel like prey.

"I'm going to take you now," he whispered in her ear. She nodded her head, her body still buzzing from energy she thought she didn't have. "I'm going to make you mine."

He positioned himself over her and gave her another smile. From there, he gently pushed inside of her.

At that moment, Elle sat straight up in her bed, her body slick with sweat, and her core thrumming with desire. She knew she would not be able to sleep at all that night.

CHAPTER SEVEN

When Glenda came to see if she needed any help dressing for breakfast the next morning she was shocked to see Elle already up and dressed, and sipping a cup of coffee. Something must have happened, usually she slept right up until her alarm clock and even hit snooze a time or two.

"Good morning, Your Highness. I trust you slept well? I have your agenda for the day and the King requests your presence for lunch today." Glenda stated as she handed Elle the folder with her list of lessons, meetings and of course, the next date on the list.

"Great, thanks Glenda. I don't suppose there is a spare moment in the schedule where I can catch a nap?" Elle reached up to massage her temples, after a fitful night of sleep after that odd dream she had she could feel a migraine hovering on the edges of her consciousness.

"There might be a spare moment after the luncheon with your father and before your lesson in planning a state dinner." Elle's eyes nearly rolled back in her head at the lesson title. "I know Your Highness, it does sound terribly boring doesn't it?"

Elle chuckled as she took a sip of her coffee, "I think I would rather go have a root canal than go through something like that, but I guess being Queen isn't all rainbows and unicorns right?"

Glenda nodded perceptibly, as she bustled around the room picking up things to be sat out for the upstairs maid to take down to the laundry. "Too right, Your Highness. Is there anything else I can get you this morning?"

"No, I think I'm just going to finish my coffee and then go check in with my mother and see what she has going on today. Do you happen to know where she is?"

"I believe I heard her mention that she was going to the rose garden." Glenda said after thinking a minute.

"Thanks Glenda, if anything pops up that needs my attention just let me know." Elle murmured as she poured another cup of coffee and set about adding a splash of cream. Glenda nodded as she took her leave and quietly closed the door behind her.

Elle spent the next few minutes reflecting on that dream, she could still feel the ghost of Simon's caress against her skin. She wasn't entirely sure what that meant, she was attracted to him yes, but she felt pulled in two directions. He was supposed to be her family's mortal enemy, but yet here she was, yearning to feel his touch. Why did dating have to be so difficult?

She sighed as she leaned down to pull her shoes on and made to leave her room, some things in life just didn't make much sense to her.

As she made her way down the corridors of the palace it was truly a feast for the senses. The priceless artwork, and vases and portraits of the past monarchs. She was lost in her thoughts and didn't realize she was standing at the doorway heading out into the garden. She pressed open the door and took a step out into the fragrant air. She wasn't quite sure where her mother was in the massive labyrinth but she figured she would take time to stop and smell the roses as the old adage goes, and maybe she would stumble across her mother along the way.

She had just reached the end of the pink rose segment and was standing there looking at the statue of her grandmother. A voice coming from her left startled her.

"Penny for your thoughts, Your Highness?" A silky smooth voice said, and immediately the butterflies took wing in her belly.

Simon was looking quite dashing this morning, dressed in a dove gray shirt and a pair of black slacks, he was twirling a red rose in between his fingers.

Elle smiled before responding, "I'm not sure they are worth that much,"

"Can I interest you in taking a walk with me this morning?" Simon said winningly as he handed her the rose.

Elle lifted the rose to her nose and gently sniffed the fragrant bloom. "I was told my mother was out here, and I was going to tour the garden with her. Besides, we aren't supposed to interact a lot outside of our scheduled events."

"While I am all for playing by the rules, I would say spending more time with you would be worth whatever consequences they put forth. That being said, I passed your mother and the King heading back inside the palace when I was walking out here. They told me where to find you."

"Well, then it appears I have an opening in my schedule, I won't tell if you won't?" Elle said with a mischievous look on her face. She tucked the rose up in her hair, and gestured to the path to the right. "After you."

With a grin, Simon gallantly offered her his arm and they set off. They spent the better part of an hour just walking and talking about their likes and dislikes, favorite books, and what they were binge watching on Netflix. As they made it back to the doorway leading into the palace, Elle was studying him intently. She wondered what his lips would feel like pressed to hers. Just then they locked gazes, and the chemistry between them surged, it was almost a visceral force when Simon stepped forward.

"I know I said I didn't like to play by the rules, but I'm dying to know what it feels like to kiss you. So I'll beg for forgiveness later, if you just allow me this one mercy."

And with that, he clasped her chin and tilted her head up and his lips descended upon hers. Elle's lips parted on a gasp and Simon took full advantage.

CHAPTER EIGHT

*W*hen Simon ripped away from her so they could breathe, Elle took the opportunity to gather herself. She needed to step back, to clear the air, or else things were going to get heated. Or else she wouldn't be able to stop.

She tried to swallow but she couldn't. Her throat was raw and rough, like sandpaper. She sucked in a breath and then another.

She picked her eyes up so they could lock with Simon's. They were hooded, dark, and filled with lust.

"I should," she said, still unable to catch her breath. "Go. I should go." Her eyes darted to the door.

"Yeah."

He nodded once. His hands clutched his hips, afraid if he released them they might run up and down Elle's body. He took a step back and he waited. Elle was relieved to know she wasn't the only one affected by the kiss. She was certain she didn't have the same experience Simon did when it came to this, but to see he was just as affected as she was reassured her of her feelings. Something was different. There was a spark between them, a spark that caused burning sensations to course through her body. A spark that was too tempting to resist.

"So I'll see you tomorrow?" Elle still tried to find her voice, and make it come out normal. She took a step forward and then another until she reached the door. It was difficult to do. It was lead, it was cement, it had roots reaching deep into to the ground.

She didn't want to leave.

She turned. She didn't even know what she was going to say. She didn't know if it would matter or not. All she knew was that she was buying time.

"Tell me." Simon seemed to know she didn't want to go. He followed her to the door, but there was still distance between them. Neither of them trusted each other to get closer. "Tell me to stay away and I will. Tell me you want to leave, and I'll walk you to your room myself. But tell me you want to stay." He took a step forward, eyes burning with a fierce intensity. She couldn't look away even if she wanted to. "Tell me you want to stay, and I won't stop. I wouldn't be able to. You've bewitched me. I don't know how, and I don't care." He stepped forward and leaned down. His head gently grazed her forehead and his lips – those delicious lips she wanted on her own again – so close to her face. All she needed to do was tilt her cheek to the side and they'd be on her again. "Tell me, Elle. Tell me what to do and I'll do it."

"I want," she said, her voice breathy and out of her control. "I want to stay."

Before she could even get the word out, Simon crashed his lips onto hers, backing her up so she hit the door behind her, there was a sitting room that was rarely ever used, just to the left of the doorway they just came in from.

50

His arms wrapped around her body, his lips warring with hers. She battled with his, opening her mouth the instant she felt his tongue teasing her bottom lip. He didn't hesitate. He plundered her offered mouth, sweeping in and tasting all that he could. His fingers pressed against her back, but she didn't care. Even if she woke up with bruises, she didn't care. She wanted it.

Elle raised her hands in his hair, feeling the silky locks between her fingers. She wanted more of this. She gently tugged his hair on his scalp, and he moaned in her mouth. Her nipples hardened at the sound and she pushed into him even more, needing to be even closer to him.

Finally, they pulled apart for air again, but their mouths were close together, as though they were sharing oxygen.

She rubbed her lips together and slowly began to unbutton his shirt. Her fingers shook. Unlike her dream, she couldn't internalize her nervousness. It made itself known. She fumbled with the first button, but he waited patiently. One quick glance, and she noticed his eyes were still dark, still filled with lust, but there was more to it. He was being patient.

This moment was important for him just as much as it was for her.

Once she finished, she slid her hands underneath the shirt and pushed the shirt off until it fell to the floor. He was bare chested before her and her hands dropped, running up and down his skin, his abdomen, the tight muscles, the feel of his soft flesh. He sucked in a breath and she realized just how much power she had over him. It only encouraged her to keep at it, to keep exploring his body.

This was no dream. This was real. This was everything she imagined it would be and more.

She shyly met his eyes once more and he smiled at her.

Her knees nearly gave out and she fell into him. He caught her with ease, sweeping her into another passionate kiss. During the kiss, his hand began to expertly unbutton the back of her shirt. Her breathing hitched and her eyes snapped open. She practically pulled away, but not completely.

"It's okay," he told her, rubbing his hand on her bare skin, trying to calm her nerves. "We can stop if you want to stop. We don't have to go any further."

"No, I." She rubbed her lips together. This wasn't going the way she planned it. Finally, she decided the best thing to do was just be honest with him. "I've never done this before. I don't know if I'm doing it the right way and I just, I don't want to mess it up."

"That's not possible," he whispered. He gave her a lingering kiss, and Elle immediately felt reassured. When he pulled away, his eyes never left hers. "We'll go slow. Anytime you're hesitant, anytime you want to change your mind, just tell me, and I'll stop. I promise."

Her dream flashed back to her. She knew it was silly to expect things to work out the same way it did in her dream, but Simon there had been considerate and gentle. She hoped that would mean Simon in reality would be the same. If anything, she was willing to trust him.

He began to undress her further, slowly as to not scare her away. She swallowed. Her throat was dry. She sucked in a breath and forgot to release it. Her chest grew tight.

It wasn't long before they were both naked, wrapped up in each other's arms. Elle slowly felt herself relax. Each time she kissed him, each time he kissed her, she gave part of her fear away piece by piece. When he moved them to the bed, she got a strange sense of déjà vu, as though she had been here before – which she had.

Her dream had prepared her for this moment.

Her dream wanted her to know that it was okay.

When she came to this conclusion, she relaxed. She felt his hardness pressing into her hip, but she was not ashamed of her desire to feel it the way she might have been previously. Instead, she looked up at him, locked eyes with him, hoping he understood that she trusted him completely. She wanted this. She wanted him. And she wasn't going to pretend otherwise.

Finally, he positioned himself, so he was hovering over her, so his desire for her caressed the top of her thigh. She knew this was the moment. He continued to look at her, a question in his eyes. She nodded, giving him permission.

He pushed inside of her slowly. Unlike her dream, pain shot through her body and she clawed at his back. This was what she was told to expect, and yet, now that it was here, she couldn't help but be shocked.

"It's okay," he murmured. "I'll wait. It's okay."

She nodded her head. She wasn't able to speak just yet. She blinked the tears from her eyes and breathed in a shallow breath before she was finally able to calm her body down. The tension was gone.

He had been patient enough to wait it out.

"I'm okay," she told him.

He nodded and began to move inside of her. He groaned with pleasure and started to mutter things under his breath about how good she felt and how he didn't want to stop. Soon, there was no pain left for her to feel. She dug her nails into his back, pushing him closer. Her pelvis thrummed with energy and it wasn't long before she felt herself reach her peak.

"I'm going to –"

Elle couldn't even finish her thought. Her desire peaked

and crashed, contracting around his desire helplessly. He held onto her and kissed her face everywhere, not missing a thrust. It wasn't long before he soon followed, spilling himself inside of her.

Once he finished, he rolled off of her, gathered her in his arms, and kissed the crown of her head. It wasn't long before she fell blissfully asleep.

CHAPTER NINE

*E*lle stretched languorously, she heard a low chuckle from next to her. Her eyes snapped open and she met Simon's amused gaze. "I was wondering how long you were going to sleep. We should probably consider getting a move on before someone gets suspicious about why the door to the sitting room is locked and it sounds like a bear is settling in for his winter's nap. " He grinned as her face took on a shocked expression.

"Do you think anyone noticed us missing?" she said as she began fumbling around putting her clothes back on.

Simon sat up and began searching for his clothes, she turned around so he could help her button up the back of her shirt.

"Elle, I'm not ashamed of what just happened, and I really hope you're not either. The camera crew and everyone will pick up on the fact that something is different. So we might as well come clean. I want to be with you, come what may." He pressed a gentle kiss to her shoulder as he fastened the last button and turned her to face him.

"I don't regret anything, but I do know that they have this show all planned out, and they expect us to see it through to the end. Despite how much I wish it would all be over, I don't want to have to keep up the façade any longer."

"Why don't you speak with your father, I bet he can convince the powers that be to call the whole thing off." he said as he sat on the settee and pulled on his boots.

She attempted to smooth her hair into some semblance of order, and looked over her shoulder at him. "Do you think he would?" It seemed like it was such an easy task, he was the leader of the country after all. Shouldn't what he says goes? But with her being a practical unknown to the people she was expected to lead soon and the positive PR that the show and her journey to finding love would provide she wasn't sure if her father would call the whole thing off.

"Ready to face the firing squad?" Simon said with a mischievous gleam in his eyes. She gulped in response, and took a tentative step forward and very nearly tripped on the lush rug. She would have fell to the ground if it wasn't for Simon catching her. She chuckled lightly and patted him on the arm, "Thanks, I've got it from here."

He gave her a minute to get her feet solidly under her before stepping back. "No need to thank me, I'll always be there to catch you when you fall."

She threw her head back and a loud peal of laughter erupted from her. "Really? That's what you're going with?"

"Too cheesy?" he said with a arched eyebrow and a faux serious look etched on his classic features.

"Just a smidge," she said as she held her fingers about a millimeter apart.

"Well, it was worth a shot..."

She smiled as she opened the door and they stepped out into the corridor. As soon as they turned the corner they very nearly ran smack into her parents. Elle felt heat rise to her cheeks, her parents both looked surprised to see them.

"Elle, Prince Simon. Just who we were looking for, where have you two been?" her father boomed.

Elle felt like she was a deer caught in the headlights, words failed her, and she shot Simon an anxious look. He smiled at her father, "Why hello Your Highness, we had just spent a lovely hour walking around the garden and talking. Your daughter is quite the conversationalist."

Elle's mother smiled as she stepped over to her daughter and took her arm, "I feel like we haven't been able to spend much time together since I got here, I was going to bake some cookies for the camera crew, would you like to join me?" Elle was still trying to find a way out of the awkward conversation and thought this was a gift sent from the gods.

"Splendid, Simon and I have some business to discuss so we'll leave you ladies to it." The king clasped a hand on Simon's shoulder and the men made their way down the hall.

"He's pretty handsome, looks like he stepped right off the pages of a fairy tale." her mother grinned as the two women headed off towards the kitchen.

CHAPTER TEN

*L*ater that night Elle heard a gentle rapping on the door to her bedroom. She set down the book she was reading and made her way over to the door. She smiled when she saw who was on the other side.

Simon was standing there, nonchalantly eating one of the cookies that she and her mother had baked earlier in the day. "You won't believe what I had to promise to get that production assistant to come off of one of these cookies."

Elle laughed, shaking her head wryly. "I can only imagine, what brings you to the palace this late at night?" She stepped aside allowing Simon to enter the room and she quietly shut the door behind him. Hoping that her mother didn't open her door right then. Elle and her mother spent a lovely afternoon baking and catching up. Elle knew her mother suspected that she and Simon were more than just acquaintances.

Simon swept the crumbs off the front of his shirt and stepped over to the window seat, elegantly dropping onto the cushioned seat. "Well you see, I didn't get a good night kiss. And I realized that I couldn't let that slide, so here I am."

Elle rolled her eyes dramatically as she made her way over to him, no one would ever suspect that the serious, stoic prince would have a surplus of cheesy pickup lines. She stepped between his sprawled out legs and leaned in and pressed her lips to his. As her lips parted on a sigh he took advantage of the movement and his tongue intertwined with hers. Her pulse started hammering in her chest, every time he kissed her it was like a thousand butterflies took wing in her abdomen.

"Well, far be it from me to deprive you." She grinned impishly and took a seat next to him. "So, what did you and my father talk about this afternoon?"

He took her hand in his and looked deep in her eyes before responding. "You mainly, your father gave me the 'you break her heart, I'll wipe out your entire bloodline,' talk. Some how he picked up on our shift in relationship and asked me my intentions. We then talked about the show, and what the people expect."

She gaped at him with her mouth hung open, but curiosity reared its head. She had to admit that she was wondering about his intentions herself. She knew that just because they slept together didn't mean that he necessarily loved her, it was too soon to be throwing that word around right?

But then a lightning bolt of realization hit her, she was falling head over heels in love with him. And truth be told, she had been falling ever since she saw him for the first time. It was like her soul saw him and knew that he was the man who would become her partner in this crazy, unpredictable life. He would be her rock and she would be his, and together they would be the monarchs that this country deserved.

It felt like suddenly all of the puzzle pieces clicked into place. Something her mother said that afternoon popped into her mind. Her mother had said that when your heart knows, it just knows. And that she hoped during the course of this show and the dates she had to go on, that she would find that one. Now they just had to get through the next few weeks of the filming of the show.

She realized that he was looking at her expectantly and that she must have zoned out and missed something important. She flushed and looked down, "Sorry about that, I got lost in thought there for a minute. What did you say?"

He caressed her hand with his thumb and cleared his throat. "I asked you if you thought that we should inform the rest of the suitors that it's all for show. I don't mean to assume that I am the last man standing, and I don't want to put any pressure on you. I know you have enough going on right now, but I do know that you have came into my life and the entire world brightened."

He continued speaking and she pressed a finger to his lips, effectively halting any further words. She loved how he respected her, and wasn't trying to assume anything, but even though he was unsure of the outcome, he bravely stepped into the breach and put his feelings out there.

"You are it for me, and I know that it's soon, and it's not going to be easy putting on a show for everyone, but when it all comes down to it, I can't see my future without you in it, and I don't want to."

As the last of the words fell off of her lips his anxious expression eased and the fierce look of love in his eyes nearly made tears fall from her eyes. It was like seeing the sunrise for the first time. He put his hands on her hips and lifted her until she was straddling his lap. He placed his hands on either side of her face and tenderly kissed her. And with that kiss it felt like the beginning of their happily ever after.

Suddenly a knock resounded on her door and they broke apart, both trying to catch their breath. Elle gingerly extracted herself from his embrace and went to see who was knocking on her door. When she pulled the door open she looked around confusedly, there was nobody there.

On the carpet right in front of her door was a envelope. On the front her name was hastily scrawled in a blood red ink. She examined the seal but didn't recognize who's it was. "What is it?" Simon said as he made his way over to her.

"I'm not sure, why would someone leave an envelope outside of my door. I thought all correspondence went through Glenda?" Elle slid her finger under the seal and opened the envelope, there was a single sheet of paper inside. The paper trembled in her fingers as she read the message it contained. Right as the paper slipped from her fingers she met Simon's gaze as he picked up the paper from the floor.

"You will marry Sir Quincy or war will break out in Procilla. Don't speak of this message to anyone, or we will know. You don't want to be the queen who leads to the downfall of an entire country. We'll be watching." Simon read the missive out loud, his voice taking on an sharp edge.

"Who's behind this?" her voice trembled as she cast her anxious gaze around the room. Someone knew that her and Simon's relationship had changed, but who was it? The only people who had seen them together were her parents, and they wouldn't do something like this. Someone had to have been watching them. Had they been spied on when they were making love? Neither of them had seen anyone in or around the sitting room, the curtains had been drawn over the windows. Unease crept down her spine.

"I will discover who is behind this, I refuse to let intimidation back us into a corner. I love you, and you love me and that's all that matters." He was pacing around the room, pulling out his phone and typing furiously.

"Say it again," she murmured, he looked up from his phone and allowed the paper to hit the floor as he strode over to where she was standing.

"I love you, Elle. Now, forever, and all of the days of our lives. We are not going to let this scum win. We need to speak with your father and his security team, my security team is en route. Let's hope the King doesn't mind getting woke up in the middle of the night."

Elle wasn't sure who was watching them, but she knew one thing for certain, a Queen didn't bow to intimidation. So she pulled herself to the tallest height she could manage, and walked purposefully across the hall to her father's bedroom door and lifted her hand to knock. After a few minutes the King opened the door, blinking confusedly.

"Elle, Simon? What in blue blazes is going on?"

"We've got a traitor in our midst." Elle murmured.

Thank You For Reading!

Don't forget to sign up for
Mind Flow Publishing & Production LLC's Newsletter @
www.mindflowpublishingproduction.com
Email us for autographed or additional paperback copies @
mindflowpubpro@gmail.com

Other Titles Also Available Include:

Mental Interlude—Poetry
The Mary B Chronicles 1- 4—Fiction
Journey to Living (Kindle Only) —Inspirational
Simple Complexity—Poetry
Spoken From The Heart—Poetry
Dreams Do Come True (Kindle Only) —Fiction
Charisma's Homecoming—Fiction
For Her Love—Fiction
Falling In Love With Poetry—Poetry
A Chance at Love—Contemporary Romance

Available Through:

Amazon
Barnes & Noble
Kindle

COMING SOON!

Freedom In The Cage Series—Fiction
Flint
Steel
Brick
Stone
Finding Kate—Suspense Thriller

Upcoming Titles Will Be Available Through:

Amazon
Barnes & Noble
Kindle
Apple iBooks
Kobo

After experiencing a tragic loss, tech billionaire Flint Marshall was hurtling head-long down a path to self-destruction. One night during an altercation he was saved by the owner of a nearby gym. Stone challenges him to put his grief to more positive uses and join their group of elite MMA fighters.

Jade had treated Flint the night he was beaten down, the ex-solider, turned trainer was tough as nails, but even she could be affected by the pain she saw reflected in Flint's eyes. When Flint joins the team and starts training for an upcoming fight, she cannot avoid the feelings he stirs inside of her.

When a client throws a curveball and disrupts the normal easy-going vibe of the gym and puts people at risk. Will Jade and Flint find their way on the path of romance, or shake hands and come out swinging?

ABOUT THE AUTHOR

Although I am still considered new to the publishing world, I have hit the ground running full speed ahead. In my first year, I was signed to Mind Flow Publishing & Production LLC, and I have published a total of 6 books. I have earned Amazon's Best Sellers Top 100 orange banner. My works are spread across several genres such as Poetry, Inspirational, Urban Fiction and Christian Fiction. I will be trying my hand at cozy mysteries, romance, and suspense thrillers. My love for writing started when I was about 12, writing poetry and writing speeches for various oratorical contests. Inspiration for my craft is pulled from my own life experiences, as well as others. I have been featured on several podcasts, as well as Up and Coming Authors Newsletters. When I am not writing, I love to design shadowboxes, and create personalized greeting cards. I have released my 3rd poetry book (Spoken from the Heart) in August 2019. Some of my current books available are The Mary B Chronicles 1-4, Mental Interlude, and Journey to Living, Simple Complexity, Dreams Do Come True, Spoken from the Heart, For Her Love and Charisma's Homecoming. All of which are available on Amazon, and www.mindflowpublishingproduction.com.